GRANDPA GUS'S BIRTHDAY CAKE

by Jan Wahl
pictures by John Wallner

Prentice-Hall, Inc.
Englewood Cliffs, New Jersey

Prentice-Hall International, Inc., London
Prentice-Hall of Australia, Pty. Ltd., North Sydney
Prentice-Hall of Canada, Ltd., Toronto
Prentice-Hall of India Private Ltd., New Delhi
Prentice-Hall of Japan, Inc., Tokyo
Prentice-Hall of Southeast Asia Pte. Ltd., Singapore
Whitehall Books Limited, Wellington, New Zealand

10 9 8 7 6 5 4 3 2 1

Library of Congress Cataloging in Publication Data
Wahl, Jan.   Grandpa Gus's birthday cake.
SUMMARY: When Grandpa Gus leaves his family who make
him feel unwanted, their shame induces them to launch a
birthday celebration.
[1. Grandfathers—Fiction.   2. Birthdays—Fiction]
I. Wallner, John C., ill.   II. Title.
PZ7.W1266Grn 1981 [E]   81-7368
ISBN 0-13-363325-X   AACR2

For Barbara Francis
with Love

Mr. and Mrs. Pipkin and
their children Bumps and Teeny
all live in this warm,
comfortable house
near the dark woods.

Grandpa Gus lives there too.
He has a nice small room
at the back of the house.

"Now keep busy, Grandpa Gus.
Stay out of my way,"
said Mrs. Pipkin one day
as she made cocklebur cookies.

"Now keep busy, Grandpa Gus.
Stay out of my way,"
said Mr. Pipkin as he
planted lettuce in the garden.

"Now keep busy, Grandpa Gus.
Stay out of our way,"
said Bumps and Teeny as
they played hopscotch.

"Turnips and tarnation!"
yelled Grandpa. "*I* can bake
cocklebur cookies!
I can plant lettuce!
I can play hopscotch!
I don't want to sit
and twiddle my thumbs!"

But nobody seemed to listen.
So, late one night when
the family was in bed,
Grandpa Gus piled his things
into a wheelbarrow.

He left a note:

Since I am in the way, I am going to live on top of <u>LONE MOUNTAIN.</u>

I love you all,
Grandpa Gus

And off he went, pushing
the wheelbarrow
through dark scary woods.
Grandpa Gus walked all night
till at last he reached
the top of Lone Mountain.

He felt very tired
but he couldn't rest quite yet.
"I'll show them
how I keep busy,"
Grandpa Gus muttered.

By sunup he was tying
twigs together
to make himself a fine hut
to live in.

Meanwhile, the Pipkins
had just jumped out of bed.
Grandpa Gus did not come for breakfast.
Mrs. Pipkin threw thistle
flapjacks on the griddle.
They were Grandpa's favorites.

The children found the note
Grandpa left and
everyone sat at the table
with long faces.
Suddenly the house felt empty.

Up on Lone Mountain
Grandpa Gus fixed a dandelion salad.
It was delicious!
But he wished he had
someone to share it with.
Then he remembered:
"Tomorrow is my birthday.
I will have to spend it alone...."

Back at the house, the
Pipkins also remembered.
"Grandpa Gus
should not be alone
on his birthday," sighed Bumps.
"No, he shouldn't," said Teeny.

"I didn't mean to
make him feel unwanted,"
said Mrs. Pipkin.
"What can we do
to show that we miss him?"
asked Mr. Pipkin.

Mrs. Pipkin smiled.
"I will make him a cake
and we'll take it to him!"
"We will help!" shouted the children.
They mixed the batter
and frosted the cake.
The cake smelled dandy.

They placed it in a box and
tied it with a big green ribbon.
Just before the Pipkins set out,
a sudden thunderstorm shook the sky.

So, in boots and yellow slickers,
off marched the Pipkins
carrying the cake.

When they came to the trail
up Lone Mountain,
it was washed away.
"Now we must climb
the side of the mountain!"
declared Mr. Pipkin.
"Hooray!" cried Bumps and Teeny.
"Onward," said Mrs. Pipkin.

Meanwhile, Grandpa Gus was carving
faces out of acorns.
"You must have somebody
to talk to," he grumbled.
"And you miss folks
telling you that you are in the way."

In the middle of the afternoon
the Pipkins came to a steep cliff.
"Now, Hector," worried Mrs. Pipkin,
"we are so little. How will we get *up*?"
"Easy, Orilla," chirped Mr. Pipkin.
"Look. I brought paper clips
to hook us together.
And balloons—for floating."

"First," asked Teeny,
"can we have something to eat?"
"A slice of cake?" suggested Bumps.
Mrs. Pipkin thought. "Well,
it was made for eating."
So she cut one piece for each.

"What a tasty treat,"
said Mr. Pipkin, smacking his lips.
"Now we must blow up
the balloons.
Grandpa Gus is above us!"
By now the thunderstorm had stopped.

"So he is," giggled Mrs. Pipkin,
tying the ribbon back
on the box.

Up they bobbed, hitched
with paper clips.
The cake had grown lighter,
but four Pipkins had grown heavier.
They dangled and danced
while the balloons bounced and popped.

"WATCH OUT!"
They banged onto a ledge.
They were so upset
that they sat down
and had another bite to eat.
It was getting dark.

"I wonder what Grandpa Gus
is doing?" said Mrs. Pipkin,
licking frosting
off her fingers.

Grandpa Gus was hanging clothes out
on a line. Then he went over
to the faces he had whittled.
"Funny," he whispered.
"It is almost as if I can
hear you speak!"

And off he went to bed
in his hermit's hut,
dreaming that Pipkins
were calling for help.
Grandpa Gus was very lonely.

The Pipkins huddled close together
to keep warm on the ledge,
dreaming they were with him.
They almost rolled off
but because they were now nice
and fat they did not.

On Grandpa Gus's
bright birthday morning,
Mr. Pipkin grunted, "Rise and shine."
"However will we get off
this ledge?" Mrs. Pipkin fussed.
"Maybe Grandpa Gus
will hear us—" began Teeny.
"—if we sing!" finished Bumps.

Grandpa Gus leaned over
the rocks at the top of Lone Mountain.
"WHO'S MAKING THAT RACKET
SINGING HAPPY BIRTHDAY?"
"Oh, Grandpa Gus!"
"We brought you a cake!"
"But we ate it coming here!"
"We miss you!"

"If we get home—"
"—we will bake you another!"
"If we get home—"
"—we will give you a great big hug!"
"I MISSED YOU!" shouted
Grandpa so loud
that the ledge began to crumble.

"GRANDPA! WHAT SHOULD WE DO?"

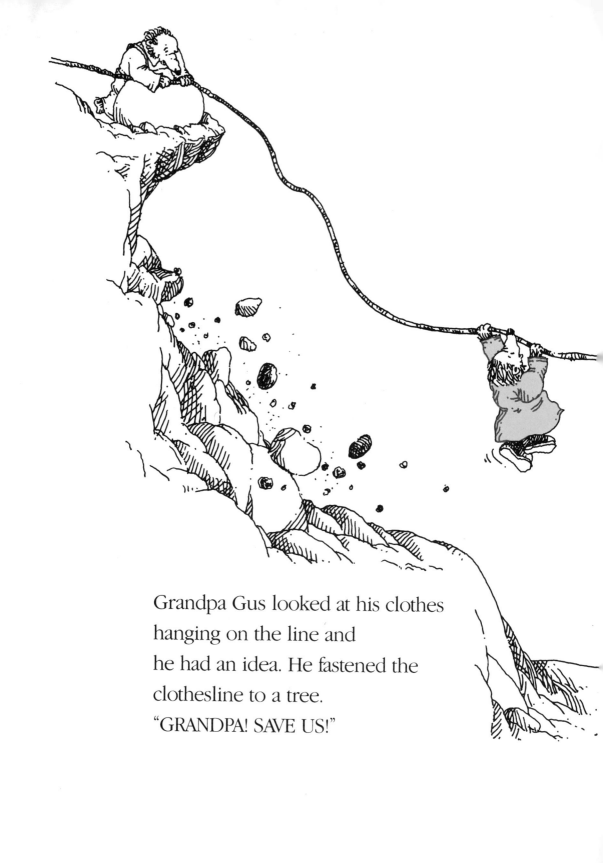

Grandpa Gus looked at his clothes
hanging on the line and
he had an idea. He fastened the
clothesline to a tree.
"GRANDPA! SAVE US!"

The clothesline arrived just in time.
Each Pipkin, Mr. and Mrs. and
Bumps and Teeny, took hold and slid
all the way to the soft mud—
whee, plop—
at the bottom of Lone Mountain.

"WHERE IS GRANDPA GUS?"
All at once down he came,
using his best pants
as a parachute.

And back home, after they washed up,
Grandpa Gus helped
bake a new birthday cake.
With mouths full of delicious crumbs,
each big and tiny Pipkin begged,
"Grandpa, please stay!"

"We'll see," winked Grandpa.